Published in the United States by Grolier Books, a division of Grolier Enterprises, Inc.

First American Edition.

ISBN: 0-7172-8466-2

WALT DISNEY'S

Sleeping Beauty

GROLIER
BOOKS

Long ago there lived a good king named Stefan.
For many years King Stefan and his queen wished
and wished for a child.

At last their wish came true. The king and queen named their daughter Aurora.

A great feast was planned to celebrate the birth of the new princess.

Everyone in the kingdom came
to the feast.

King Hubert arrived with his son, Prince Phillip.
The two kings decided that one day
Phillip and Aurora would marry.
"That way our kingdoms will
always be united," King Hubert
told his son.

Three good fairies came to the feast. Each had a special gift for the princess.

Flora waved her wand. "I give you the gift of beauty."

"My gift shall be the gift of song," said Fauna.

"And my gift . . ." began Merryweather. Suddenly a blast of wind blew open the castle doors.

A bright flame filled the room. Then the wicked fairy, Maleficent, appeared from the flame.

"You did not invite me to the feast, King Stefan. But I, too, have a gift for the princess."

Maleficent pointed at the cradle. "Before the sun sets on her sixteenth birthday, the princess will prick her finger on the spindle of a spinning wheel. And she will die!"

"Seize that creature!" shouted the king. But Maleficent disappeared in a cloud of smoke.

Luckily, Merryweather still had her magical gift to give. The good fairy could not undo the evil spell.

But she could soften it.

Merryweather waved her wand. "Sweet Aurora," she said,

Not in death, but just in sleep,
The fateful prophecy you'll keep.
From this slumber you shall wake,
When true love's kiss the spell shall break.

King Stefan had all the spinning wheels
in the kingdom burned.
"If there are no spinning wheels," he told
the Queen, "our daughter will be safe from harm."

The three
fairies knew
Aurora still
wasn't safe.

Flora had an idea. The fairies would secretly raise
the princess themselves in a cottage in the woods.
"And no magic," Flora told the others. "Then
Maleficent will never be able to find us."

The fairies explained their plan to the king and queen. Reluctantly, the king and queen agreed.

That night three peasant women left the castle with a small bundle.

The three women
arrived at a cottage
nestled deep in the forest.
"We must never call
her Princess Aurora,"
Flora told the others.
"Her new name is
Briar Rose."

Sixteen happy years passed. Briar Rose
grew into a lovely young woman.
She did not know she was a princess.

And she had
never heard of
the evil fairy.

But Maleficent had not forgotten the princess! For years her soldiers had searched the kingdom. At last they gave up.

"We checked every cradle," they told Maleficent. "Fools!" she shouted. "You've been looking for a baby all these years!"

Maleficent turned to her pet raven. "You are my last hope. Search for a maid of sixteen with hair of gold. Go, and do not fail me."

The raven flew off into the night.

The next day was Briar Rose's sixteenth birthday. The fairies wanted to surprise her with a party, so they sent her out of the cottage.

"We need berries," Fauna said.

"Lots of berries," added Flora.

"Don't hurry back," called Merryweather.

The fairies set to work.
Flora made a dress.
Fauna baked a cake.

"This dress
looks awful,"
declared
Merryweather.

The fairies
needed a
little magic.

Meanwhile, Briar Rose was singing to the forest animals. She told them all about a prince she had met in her dreams.

Nearby, Prince Phillip was riding his horse. When he heard Briar Rose singing, the prince couldn't resist joining in.

For a little while they sang and danced together.

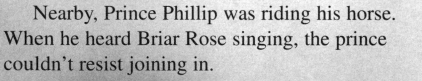

"What is your name?" Prince Phillip asked.

"Why, it's . . ." Just then, Briar Rose remembered that she was not allowed to talk to strangers. "I have to go," she said quickly.

"When will I see you again?" asked the prince. He had already fallen in love with Briar Rose.

"Tonight. I live in the cottage in the glen," she called as she hurried away.

Back at the cottage, Fauna had fetched their magic wands. She waved her wand. Now the cake was perfect!

Flora changed the dress she had made into a beautiful pink gown.

"It should be blue," said Merryweather. She made the dress blue.

"Pink!" shouted Flora.

The fairies kept changing the dress from pink to blue and blue to pink. Pink and blue magic dust flew everywhere!

Maleficent's raven saw the magic dust flying out of the chimney. He had found the princess! Back he went to tell Maleficent.

Just then, Briar Rose returned to the cottage.

"Surprise!" the fairies shouted.

"Oh, this is the happiest day of my life!" cried Briar Rose. "I met the most wonderful young man. He's coming here tonight."

The fairies could see she was in love.

"But that's terrible," said Fauna.

"Why?" asked Briar Rose.

The fairies told Briar Rose that she was really Princess Aurora. She had to return to the castle that very night. And she had to marry a prince.

Aurora was very unhappy. She would never see the young man she had met in the forest again.

Yet everyone in the castle was happy. King Stefan couldn't wait to see his daughter. And King Hubert couldn't wait for her to marry Prince Phillip!

When they arrived
at the castle, the fairies
left to fetch the king
and queen.

No sooner had they gone than a magic ball of
light appeared.

Aurora followed
it up the stairs
to a small room.

Maleficent was waiting for her—
with a spinning wheel!
Aurora had never seen
a spinning wheel before.
She reached for the spindle.
"Touch it," Maleficent
hissed.
Aurora touched the
spindle and fell into a
deep sleep.

The three fairies had been searching for Aurora.
They found her lying on the floor, fast asleep.

The fairies placed the princess on a bed.

"She will sleep until she is kissed by her true love," sighed Flora. "Perhaps he is the young man she met in the forest."

"He was coming to the cottage tonight," remembered Merryweather.

"Let's meet him there," said Flora. "But first, let's put everyone in the castle to sleep. That way no one will know what has happened."

The fairies cast a spell
over the entire castle.
Soon everyone was
fast asleep.

Prince Phillip had already arrived at the cottage. He had decided to marry the girl he had met in the forest instead of Princess Aurora.

Maleficent's soldiers were waiting for him. They tied up the prince and brought him to the Forbidden Mountains.

Maleficent told Prince Phillip that the girl in the forest was really Princess Aurora. She was sure he would never escape to wake his sleeping beauty.

But the three
fairies realized what
had happened.
They sneaked into
the dungeon and
freed the prince.

"Take this magic
sword and shield to
protect you," said
Merryweather. The
prince set off to rescue
the princess.

Maleficent tried to
stop him.

She raised an enormous
hedge of
thorns around
King Stefan's
castle.

But Prince Phillip
hacked his way through
the thorns. The evil
fairy was furious!

She transformed
herself into a fire-breathing
dragon and tried to destroy
the prince. Luckily, the
magic shield protected him.

Finally the prince saw his chance. He threw the
sword at the dragon's heart. That was the end of the
dragon—and the evil fairy, too!

The prince entered
the palace yard.
Everyone was sleeping!

He raced up the stairs
to the tower.

He found Princess Aurora asleep on the bed.
As soon as he kissed her, Aurora's eyes opened.
The spell had been broken!

Everyone else
in the castle woke
up, too.

The king and queen were very happy to see their daughter. And King Hubert was very happy to learn that the prince and princess were in love!